THIS BLOOMSBURY BOOK

BELONGS TO

....

For Christy Blance, with love – JN

For Edie, Sachie and Ossie – JC

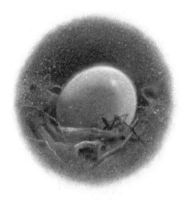

First published in Great Britain in 2002 by Bloomsbury Publishing Plc
38 Soho Square, London, W1D 3HB
This paperback edition first published in 2004

Text copyright © Judith Nicholls 2002
Illustrations copyright © Jason Cockcroft 2002
The moral rights of the author and illustrator have been asserted

A CIP catalogue record of this book is available from the British
Library

ISBN 0 7475 6908 8

Printed in China

5 7 9 10 8 6

All papers used by Bloomsbury Publishing are natural, recyclable
products made from wood grown in well-managed forests. The
manufacturing processes conform to the environmental regulations of the
country of origin.

Billywise

Judith Nicholls

illustrated by
Jason Cockcroft

BLOOMSBURY
CHILDREN'S
BOOKS

From a mole-black hole
in the oldest oak,
deep in the heart
of the fern-brushed wood …

a scritch, a scratch,
a tap, a crack!

A pale egg split …
and Billywise crept out of it.

'Who are *you*?' murmured moth
from the shadowy glade.
'You're not rough,
you're not tough,
just a small ball of fluff ...
you wouldn't make *anyone* afraid!'

'Who am I?' whispered Billywise,
safe in his shady nest.
But his mother, fondly feeding him, said,
'*Hush*! Just eat and rest!'

'You will grow, you will prowl,
you will slide through the air;
you will swoop, loop-the-loop,
you will stare, you will glare …
as silently as moonlight
you'll glide through the midnight air.'

But Billywise just blinked in fear
and whispered,
'I won't dare!'

Next night,
whilst his mother searched for food ...

'Who are *you*?' squeaked squirrel,
peering from a branch nearby.
'You can't catch me,
I'd beat you on any tree –
and it doesn't look as if *you'll* ever fly!'

'Who am I?' whispered Billywise,
huddling in his nest.
But his mother, fondly feeding him, said,
'*Hush*! Just eat and rest!'

'You will grow, you will prowl,
you will slide through the air;
you will swoop, loop-the-loop,
you will stare, you will glare …
as silently as moonlight
you'll glide through the midnight air.'

But Billywise just blinked in fear
and whispered,
'I won't dare!'

Before long there were three
in the oldest oak:
Billywise, Jennyhowlett and Pudge.

And they *grew*.

Billywise cried, '*Please*,
why are those two there?
Do I *have* to share?
This really *is* a squash and a squeeze!'

They pushed and wriggled,
they squeezed and wiggled
until, at last, they slept.

They slept all day,
then watched their mother fly away
as the sunlight stole from the wood …

And they grew!
They grew and they GREW,
and soon Billywise
dreamt of *space*.

He longed to swoop,
loop-the-loop,
to slide through the air,
as silently as moonlight
to glide through the midnight air.

But …
did he dare?

One night,
when the moon was high overhead,
Billywise stepped up to the edge of the nest,
with searching eyes and wings outspread.

And his mother said,

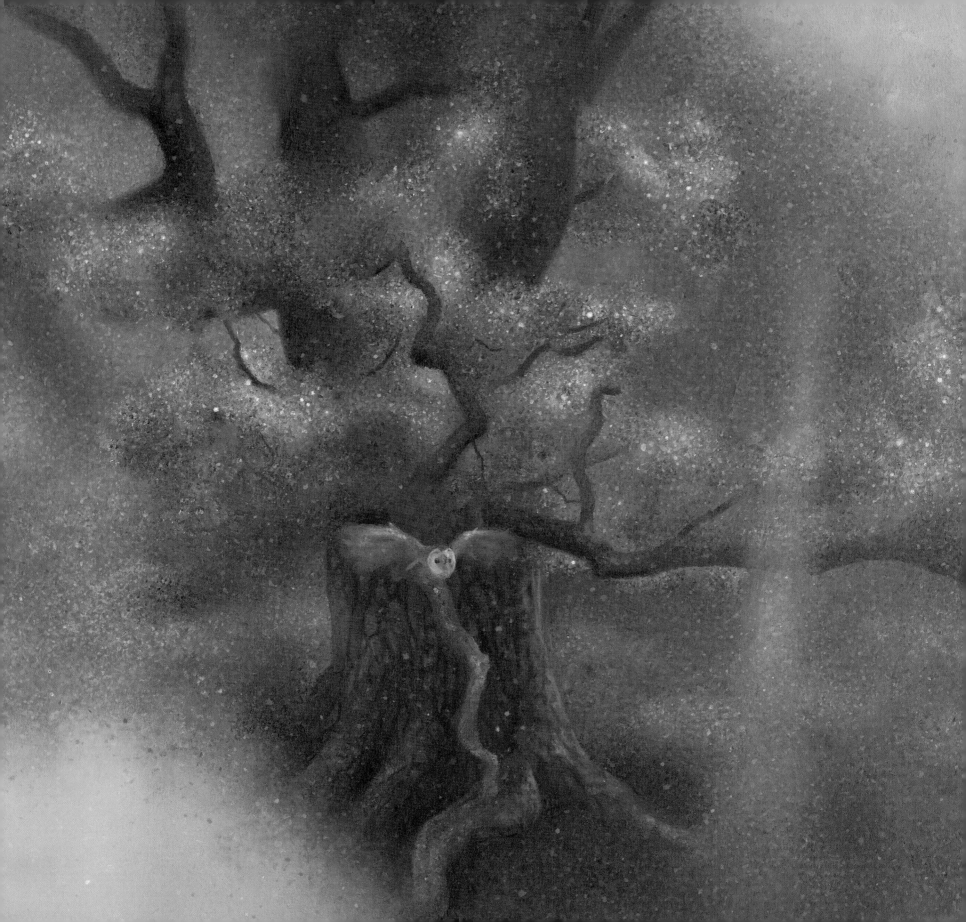

'If you tried,
you could glide!

Spread your wings to the side,
fix your ears on the night,
let the stars light your flight
and aim for the moon!'

'You're an OWL, Billywise!
You can dive, you can prowl,
you can slide through the air;
you can swoop, loop-the-loop,
you can stare, you can glare!'

'JUMP, Billywise!

As silently as moonlight,
glide through that midnight air!'

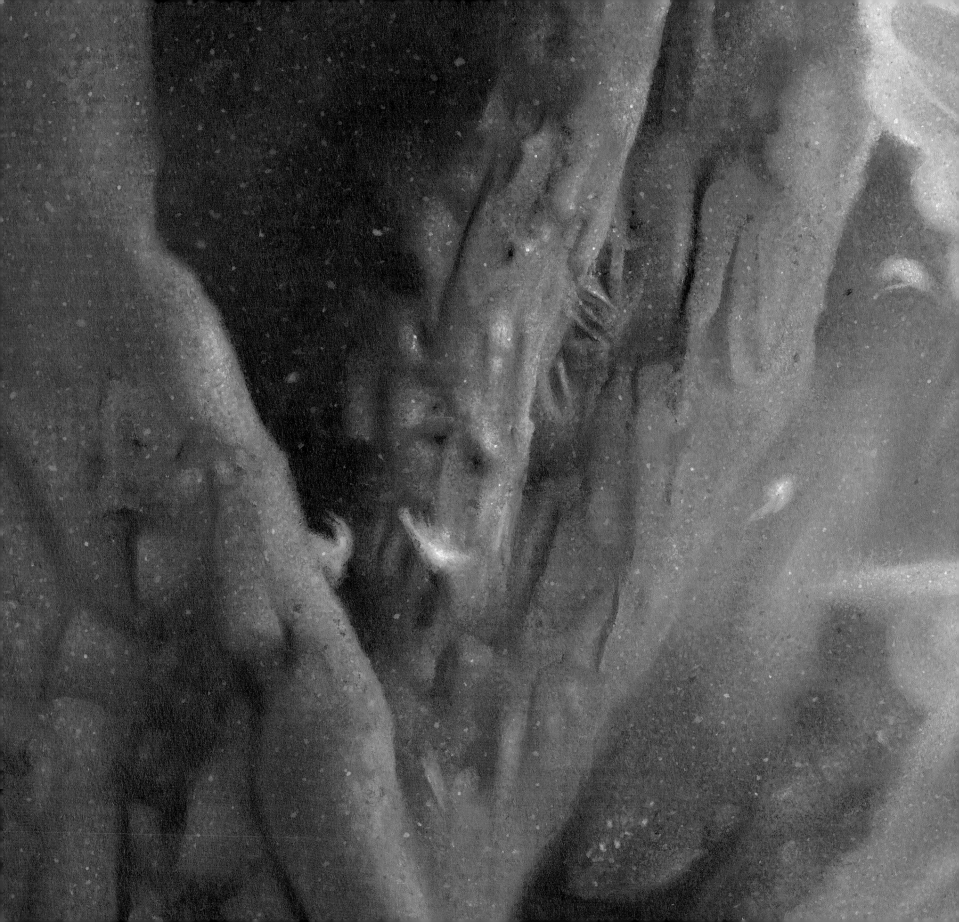

Billywise breathed deeply,
spread his wings to the watching wood
and cried,

'I'm an *owl*,
I dare, I dare!'